A Richard Jackson Book

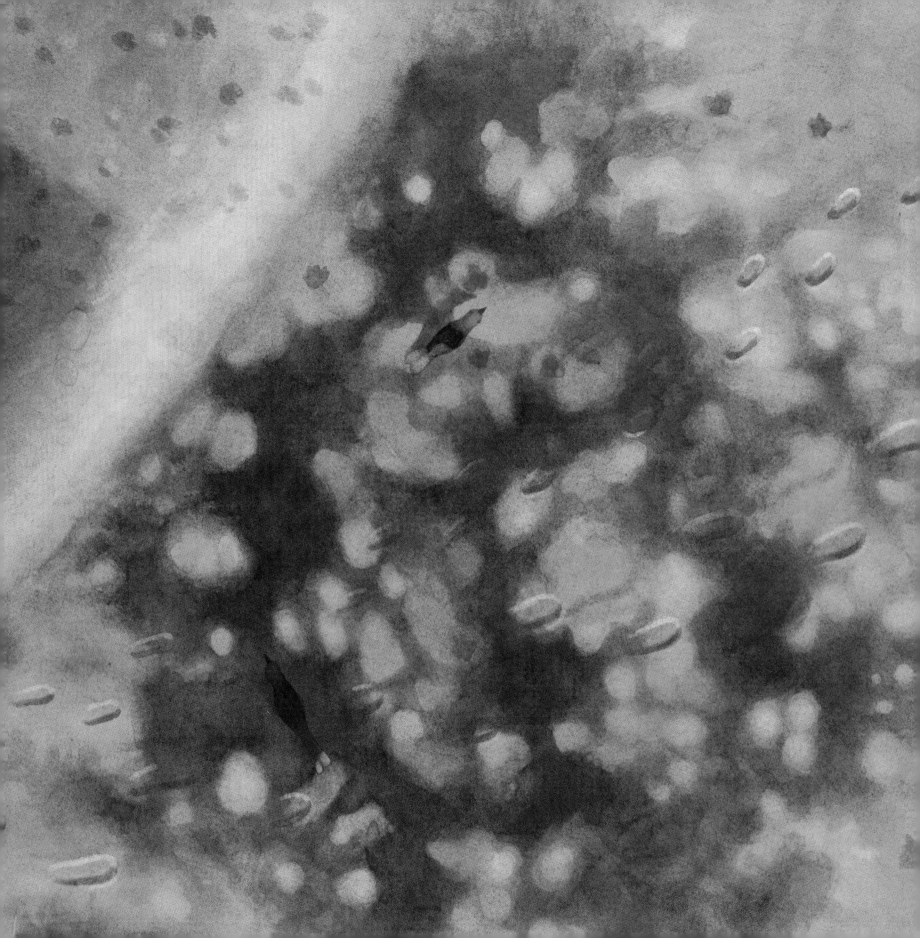

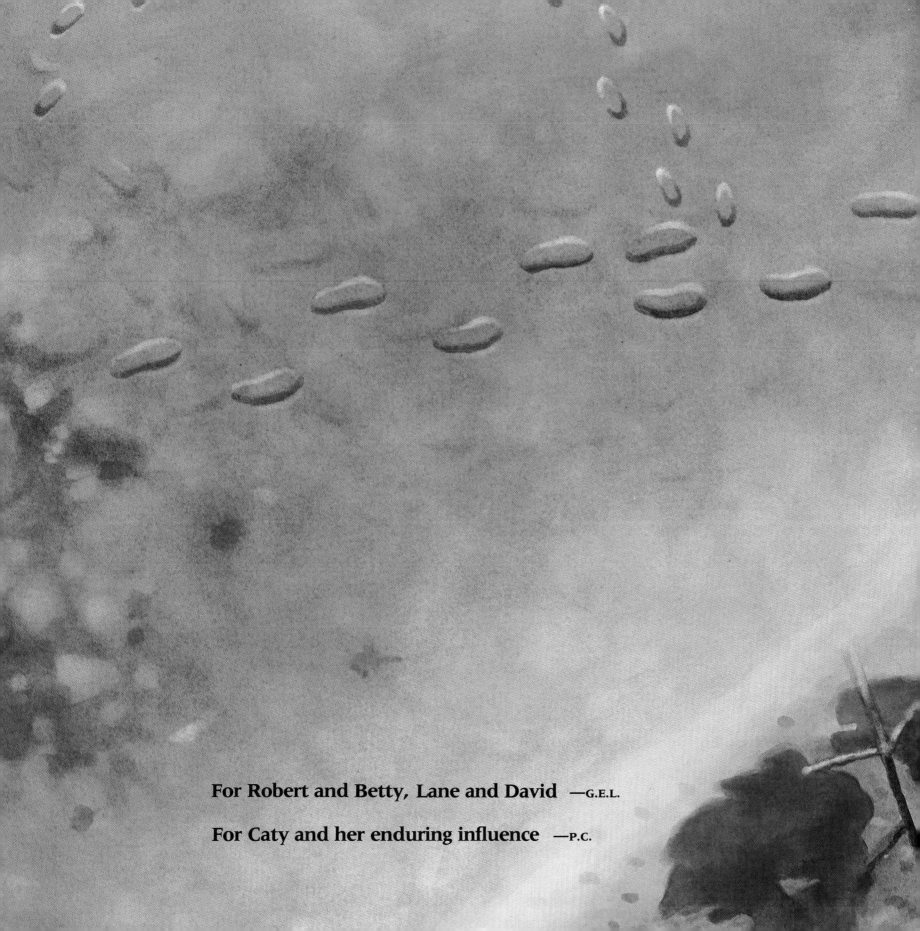

For Robert and Betty, Lane and David —G.E.L.

For Caty and her enduring influence —P.C.

See that path?

Just a trace through the woods
till it joins the blacktop down the hill,
but folks have been traveling it
thousands of years.

It's an old, old, old, old road.

Who came down that road, Mama?

Who Came Down That Road?

story by George Ella Lyon · paintings by Peter Catalanotto

ORCHARD BOOKS · NEW YORK

My great-grandma and great-grandpa,
just married and looking to farm,
they came down that road.

Who came before that, Mama?
Who came down that road?

Soldiers in blue coats,
saddle high or marching,
they came down that road.

Who came before the soldiers, Mama?

Pioneers and settlers, honey,
floating the Ohio

and clearing the wildwood,
they came down that road.

Who came before the settlers, Mama?
Who came down that road?

Shawnee and Cherokee,
Wyandot and Chippewa

in beads and feathers, following deer,
they came down that road.

Who came before the Indians, Mama?

Buffalo, bear, great-antlered elk,
to lick their fill at the flat salt lick,

they came down that road.

Who came before the buffalo?

Mastodons and woolly mammoths
plunging through forests,
trampling canebrakes
to get away from the breath of ice

and they helped make that road.

Who came before the mammoths, Mama?

Fish swam in a sea so warm
and shallow you could have waded across,
except of course there wasn't any you
when water lay over that road.

The sea left the salt lick, though.

What came before the sea?

Questions!
Questions crowded like a bed of stars,

thick as that field of goldenrod—

questions came before sea and ice,
before mastodon and grizzly bear

before Indian and pioneer,
before soldiers and newlyweds

the mystery of the making place—

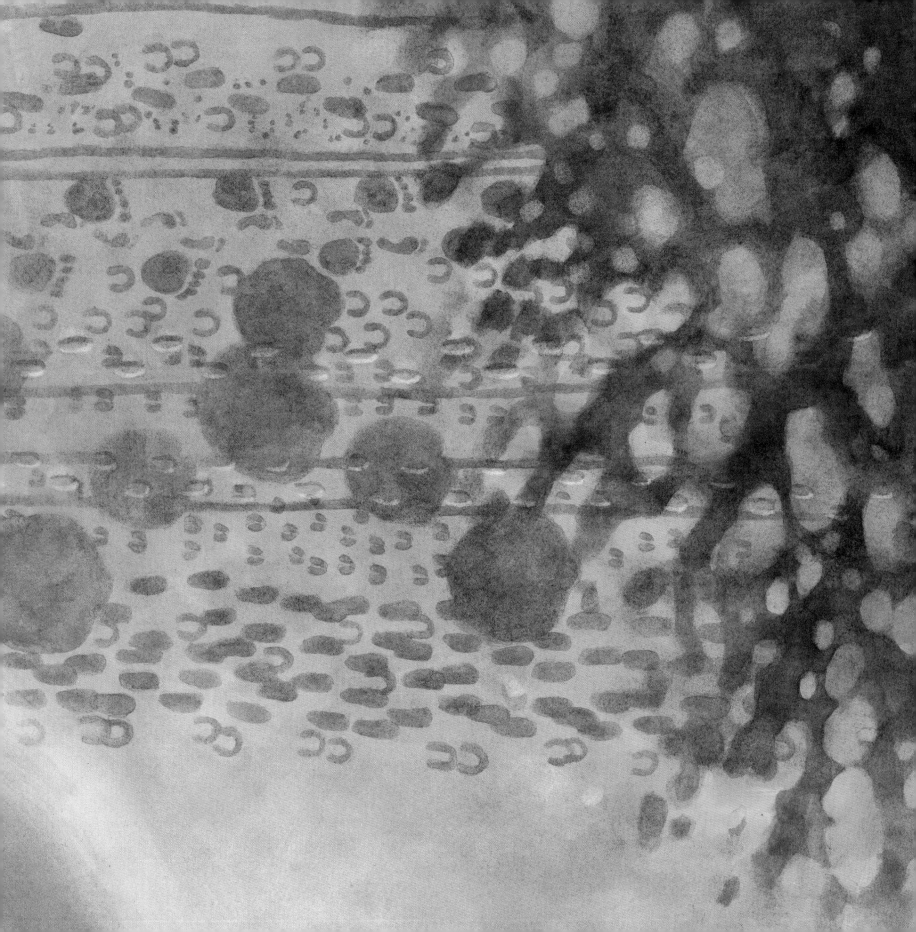

that came before this road.

Special thanks to the Lyons—P.C.

Text copyright © 1992 by George Ella Lyon
Ilustrations copyright © 1992 by Peter Catalanotto

Orchard Books, 95 Madison Avenue, New York, NY 10016

Manufactured in the United States of America. Printed by Barton Press, Inc.
Bound by Horowitz/Rae. Book design by Mina Greenstein.
The text of this book is set in 20 point Meridien Bold. The illustrations are watercolor paintings reproduced in full color.   10 9 8 7 6 5 4 3 2

Library of Congress Cataloging-in-Publication Data
Lyon, George Ella, date. Who came down that road? / story by George Ella
Lyon ; paintings by Peter Catalanotto.   p.   cm. "A Richard Jackson book."
Summary: Mother and child ponder the past in discussing who might have traveled down an old, old road, looking backwards from pioneer settlers all the way to prehistoric animals.   ISBN 0-531-05987-1.   ISBN 0-531-08587-2 (lib. bdg.)
[1. Roads—Fiction.   2. Mother and child—Fiction.] I. Catalanotto, Peter, ill.
II. Title. PZ7.L9954Wh 1992 [E]—dc20 91-20742

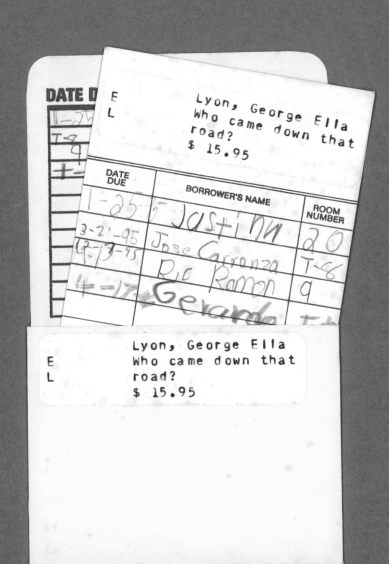

DATE D

E
L
    Lyon, George Ella
    Who came down that
    road?
    $ 15.95

DATE DUE	BORROWER'S NAME	ROOM NUMBER
1-25	Justinn	20
3-21-95	Jose Carranza	T-6
12-19-95	Ric Ramon	9
4-17-	Gerardo	T-

E
L
    Lyon, George Ella
    Who came down that
    road?
    $ 15.95